Other Books by Judy Delton

KITTY IN THE MIDDLE
KITTY IN THE SUMMER

ONLY JODY

Judy Delton

Houghton Mifflin Company
Boston   1982

Printed in the United States of America
v 10 9 8 7 6 5 4 3 2 1

Library of Congress Cataloging in Publication Data
Delton, Judy.
Only Jody.
Summary: Fifth grader Jody is the only boy in a
family with three women, and the only boy he knows named
Jody.
I. Porter, Pat Grant, ill.   II. Title.
PZ7.D3880p   [Fic]   81-20178
ISBN 0-395-32080-1   AACR2

For Mary Jo Collins, who likes what I write

ONLY JODY

1

JODY WAS THE only boy in a house with three
women. His sister Jill was sixteen and wrote
books upstairs in her room. His sister Joana was
twelve and in junior high school. His mother
was forty-four and had always wanted to be a
tap dancer. She didn't dance, but she wore tap
shoes when she watered the plants and cooked
breakfast.

People often thought Jody was a girl too. "Oh,
so you have three girls!" they would say to his
mother when they heard the names of the children. "No," his mother would explain, "Jody is a
boy." The reason that she had to explain this
was that Jody is a girl's name as well as a boy's.

Two girls in Jody's school were named Jody. His mother said that if she had it to do over again she wouldn't give all her children names starting with *J*. But what good did that do now? he wondered. He already had a name that could be mistaken for a girl's. Last week when Jody went to the doctor, the name on the prescription for allergy pills was Janice.

Jody's family had just moved to St. Paul where there were city buses so that his mother wouldn't have to drive the children "to everything." It turned out that she drove them anyway because it wasn't good to take buses alone or in the dark. But his mother insisted that they still liked the city better. Besides they had bought a house that she said they probably couldn't sell because it was crooked. "We can't have everything," she said the day they bought the house. "It has a stained-glass window and a fine fireplace."

"But it hasn't got a garage," Jody had pointed out, "and the roof is crooked."

"A fireplace and a stained-glass window are more important," she had said.

They moved in and Jody started fifth grade at Taylor School. His mother didn't like the boys he brought home from school, or the boys in the neighborhood either, so it was difficult to make friends.

"It's better to be alone than to have friends who don't suit you," she would answer when he complained. "Jill had no friends when she started high school and it turned out fine. She wrote books instead."

So Jody drew pictures of the people in his class and sold them at school for fifteen cents each until he had saved enough money to buy *Gray's Anatomy*. He wanted to be a doctor when he grew up. When his mother found out she said that was foolish since he had so much talent in art. After that, Jody read the book in his room with his door closed. Sometimes he drew the body and the muscles and tendons. His mother called it art but Jody knew that it was anatomy.

One day when Jody had been at Taylor School for several months and was getting used to it, Mr. Johnson asked how many boys would like to join the wrestling team. Jody raised his hand and signed up. Every afternoon after school, he would go to wrestling practice. When he had been wrestling for several weeks, he ran home one day to show his mother how he could flex his biceps. But when he opened the back door, he saw a note on the refrigerator under the magnets shaped like watermelon slices. It said, "Jody: I'm at Renee's. (Renee was his mother's best friend.) Make egg salad for supper. (Jody liked egg salad, it was full of protein.) I transferred you to St. Gertrude's School. Call the principal and tell him you won't be back. Love, Mom."

Jody was usually a very quiet boy, but when he read the note, he gave a war howl that could be heard clear down the block and was as loud as the drummer next door his mother complained about. He even stamped his feet and pounded on the refrigerator door, and when he still didn't feel better, he lay down on the floor and kicked his feet the way he'd seen small children do in the doctor's office when they didn't want a shot. Before long his sister Jill came down from where she was writing her book and said, "What's going on, anyway?"

"Mom's putting me in St. Gertrude's," screamed Jody.

"Oh," said Jill, taking an English muffin from the cupboard and going back up to her room.

Jody went into his room and threw himself on his bed and sulked. Just when he was getting used to Taylor. Just when he'd joined the wrestling team. That would make eight schools in his ten short years. Eight schools!

The back door slammed and Joana walked in. Jody went out to the kitchen. "What's the matter, Jo?" she asked when she saw the look on his face.

"Read the note on the refrigerator," he said.

Joana read the note and said, "Oh Jody, that's terrible." (Joana was always far more sympathetic than Jill.) "Why would Mom do that?"

Jody shook his head. He felt too awful to talk.

"What did you do?" she said. "Did you get into trouble?" Many mothers sent their children to St. Gertrude's instead of Taylor if they were "problems."

"Nothing!" shouted Jody. "What would I do? Nothing!"

"Well," said Joana practically, "we'll have to wait 'til Mom comes home and ask her."

Jody got a box of Kleenex from the bathroom and sat on the living room sofa and felt awful.

Everyone at Taylor hated St. Gertrude's. It was a Catholic school run by nuns and the students wore uniforms, wine-colored pants and light-wine-colored shirts. The boys wore black ties that had no purpose and wine-colored sweaters, if any. Jody hated uniforms. They were for sissies.

Jody knew, though, that if his mother had made up her mind, there was no use arguing. His mother meant what she said. He went to the phone and called the principal at Taylor who seemed surprised at the news. Jody was not a troublemaker.

"I don't know," Jody said, when the principal asked why he was changing schools. Jody went in and lay on his bed and tried to think of something else, but all he could think of was St. Gertrude's. Religion classes. And they didn't have wrestling. He had heard that the nuns were very strict. They gave lots of homework and everyone had to go to Mass every morning. After what seemed to be a very long time, Jody heard his mother's key in the lock.

"Jody?" she said in a very light voice, as though she was anticipating trouble but was willing to go halfway.

Jody didn't answer. He'd go to St. Gertrude's if he had to, but he wouldn't make it easy for her. He began to sniffle.

"Jo?" his mother said, coming into his room. "What are you crying about?"

"You know what I'm crying about. I don't want to go to St. Gertrude's."

His mother sat on the edge of his bed. "St. Gertrude's is a fine school," she said. "They wear uniforms and have religion classes and they will give more attention to your art talent."

"What's wrong with Taylor?" said Jody.

His mother waved her hand. "St. Gertrude's is better. You'll learn more in a private school. And it's safer," she said.

Jody had no idea of giving up. He buried his eyes in the pillow and moaned.

"I'll give you five minutes to dry your eyes and not look like you've been crying. We have an appointment at seven with Sister Rosewitha. I want

you to act like you want to go there. They don't
like it when mothers force their children to
come."

Jody's mother had gone halfway.

2

_____

WHEN THEY ARRIVED at St. Gertrude's, Jody's eyes were still red and his mother glared at him to smile and look like he wanted to be there. The convent where they met Sister Rosewitha was filled with black-robed nuns who didn't smile much themselves, he thought. Why should he smile if they didn't. While his mother was filling out the yellow papers and paying tuition and book money, Sister Rosewitha told Jody where to wait for the bus at 6:30 in the morning, and asked if he knew the Apostles' Creed.

"He will by tomorrow," said Jody's mother and then they stood up and said good-bye.

"Learn the Apostles' Creed," said Jody's

mother in the car, handing him a paper with a lot of words on it. Jody read it.

"What's 'conceived by the Holy Ghost'?"

"It means he didn't have a real father."

"Everyone has to have a father."

"God was his father."

Jody knew from his medical books that there had to be more to it than that.

"Just learn it by heart," said his mother, ending the discussion.

When Jody went to school the next day, he recited the entire Apostles' Creed for Sister Rosewitha.

"You learned that so quickly, Jody, you may begin to memorize the Act of Contrition."

This time Jody took his time memorizing because he knew that when he recited the Act of Contrition, Sister would admire his swift mind and set him to learning the acts of faith, hope, and love.

After his third day at the new school, Jody went with his mother to get his uniform. He didn't really want a uniform, but he hated being

11

the only one in the room without one. Sitting in his brown corduroys and ski sweater among the sea of wine made him feel very conspicuous indeed. Jody already felt conspicuous belonging to a family with three women. He didn't want to feel conspicuous in school too. So he didn't complain when his mother made him try on the new stiff wine-colored pants and the polyester wine shirt and the black tie. He took off his tennis shoes and put on the brown oxfords. He felt conspicuous in the store and on the street, but he felt right at home after that at St. Gertrude's.

Several mornings later when Jody woke up and looked out the window, he noticed that there was snow on the ground. It would be great fun, he thought, to slide on the ice in his brown oxfords. They had slippery leather soles, which was the only good thing he could say about them. He'd wear a smooth path all the way down the hill to the bus. He might even be able to slide from the top to the bottom without walking in between at all. This possibility excited him enough so that he hurriedly got dressed and made his bed and put his anatomy book away. It had fallen onto the floor when he went to sleep the night before. He hummed a tune from Joana's latest record even though he didn't like music. He had to admit that St. Gertrude's wasn't quite as bad as he had expected. Even oxfords could be good for something. He heard his mother's tap shoes on the kitchen floor, and the smell of corned beef drifted into his room. His mother often made Reuben sandwiches for breakfast. She had read somewhere that they (and pizza) included all the necessary food groups to qualify as a nutritious breakfast. Although he never said anything, Jody thought Reuben sandwiches made a better lunch. He preferred oatmeal or bacon and eggs for breakfast.

"Hi Jody," his mother said as he came into the kitchen. She set a large Reuben sandwich before him. "Did you see that it snowed out? Looks like winter's here. Get your warm jacket out, and wear a cap." His mother poured him a glass of milk. "Have you got mittens? You'll need mittens today."

Jody nodded. He had mittens that made fine round snowballs. He ate his sandwich and cleared the table, then went to his room to get his books together and his warm clothes on. Just as he was about to go out the door, his mother called, "Your boots, Jody, don't forget your boots."

"I don't need boots," said Jody, feeling his spirits fall.

"Of course you need boots with those shoes," said his mother. "You can't walk through all that snow with just dress shoes on, you'll have wet feet and you'll slip and fall."

Jody clenched his fists and felt like crying. His mother clicked up the basement steps and handed him his boots. Joana's boots. Any boots were bad enough. But these were girls' boots, with zippers instead of buckles. It seemed as if everything he'd worn all his life (except his uniform) had belonged to girls. His mother always said, "There's no difference, Jody. It's all in your head" and "This is just like new, we aren't going to get rid of it and buy you something almost the same."

Almost. That was the word. Almost meant a lot. These boots might be black rubber, but they were definitely not boys' boots.

"Hurry up, you'll miss your bus." She kissed him good-bye and went back to bed. Jody sat down and pulled on the boots. He wished he had enough money to buy his own. But he knew what his mother would say even if he did: "Money isn't the issue, Jody, you don't need new boots."

Jody pulled his wine-colored pants down over the boots hoping they would look like shoes. He got outside and ran down the hill for a long slide. The boots didn't move. They gripped the snow underfoot and held on like magnets. Thud, thud, thud. Even when he came to solid ice, the boots refused to move. It was almost as though they had glue on the bottom.

At school Jody kicked them off into the cloak-room, wishing he never had to see them again. He hung up his jacket and cap, then stood to salute the flag and say morning prayers with the class. When Sister Rosewitha gave the spelling test all Jody could think about was boots. Otto, the boy across the aisle from Jody, asked him how many *C*'s *occasion* had. Jody whispered two. Jody could spell anything, even medical words.

At three o'clock when the bell rang, Jody got up with the rest of the class to get his jacket and cap. Since it was the first snow day of the year almost everybody was holding up mittens that had lost a mate. Sister Rosewitha was waving a green mitten from the front of the room. "Who has a green mitten like this?" she called. "Karen has only one mitten. Will you look and see if you have it please?" Mary had the mitten.

Then Sister Rosewitha gave a lecture on having names in mittens and boots. Suddenly Claudia waved her hand. "Sister, Sister, I have the wrong boot. This one is like mine, but it's the wrong size."

Sister sighed. She walked down and took the boot from Claudia and held it up in the front of the room. "Girls," she said. "This is exactly my

point. So many girls wear the same kind of boots, it is impossible to identify them without your name inside. Who has Claudia's boot? Will each girl please check right now and see if she has one boot that does not belong to her?"

All of the girls checked. Jody had one of his boots on. When he began to put the other on, it wouldn't go over his shoe. He pulled and pulled. It wouldn't go on. He slapped his forehead with the palm of his hand. "Oh, no!" he said to himself. Sister was still waving the boot in front of the room. "Girls," she said. "Who has Claudia's boot?" The girls were shaking their heads. All of them except Claudia had their boots on and were sitting in their seats sideways with scarves around their faces and lunchboxes in their hands waiting for the second bell to ring.

"Sister! Sister!" cried Otto. "Jody has the wrong boot!" Otto's eyes were big and round and eager with discovery. He liked to solve problems. A real Sherlock Holmes, thought Jody.

Jody wished he were dead. He wished he'd never come to St. Gertrude's. He wished he could fall through the floor, or out the window, or disappear into a gray mist. But nothing like that happened; it was very quiet and every girl in the room was looking at him. And now, he was sure, every boy.

"Jody?" Sister was saying, out of the silence, "Is this your boot?"

Jody wanted to yell out that he'd never seen it in his life, that he'd never worn that boot. Otto was pulling on his jacket. "Go get your boot," he was saying, happy to have solved the mystery.

"Here is Claudia's boot, Sister," said Otto, picking the boot up from the floor where Jody had dropped it. He walked to the front of the room with it and Claudia, smiling in relief, came to claim it. It was so quiet, all that could be heard was the ticking of the clock. Jody sat, red-faced, aware of the smell of damp wool and rubber and the tick of the clock. "I'll take it to him," said Otto, on the way back to his seat.

Now whispering replaced the stillness. Jody knew they were whispering about him. About a boy who would wear girls' boots. The second bell rang and everyone forgot about Jody's boots except Jody. They dashed to line up at the door and get out into the snow and slide on the way home.

Jody put on the boot without saying a word. Otto was waiting for him. Why doesn't he go? thought Jody. What is he hanging around for? To laugh at me? But when he stood up he saw that Otto wasn't laughing after all. He was pulling up his pants legs to show Jody his boots. Jody looked. They didn't have buckles, either. They were, of all things, girls' boots!

"Are those your sister's boots?" said Otto. "My mom makes me wear my sister's boots too. 'There's a lot of wear left in those, Otto.'" He mimicked his mother's mincing tones.

Jody couldn't hide his surprise. He hadn't thought there was another mother in the world like his. Not anywhere.

Well, he said to himself. Otto probably doesn't eat corned beef for breakfast.

3

JODY DECIDED THAT if he was ever to have friends,
Otto would be the one to start with. Someone
whose mother made him wear his sister's boots to
school would understand Jody's own mother if
anyone could. Not that Jody needed friends. He
had lots of things to do every day — like cleaning
up his room, drawing, reading his medical book,
flexing his biceps. But it was no fun to be alone all
the time, even though his mother said it would
make him creative. So all the next week at school
he thought about asking Otto over to his house.
One night he circled all the days on the calendar
when he knew his mother wouldn't be home, and

the next day at recess he asked Otto if he wanted to come over and see his coin collection.

"I'll call my mom and ask her," said Otto. Jody went along to the principal's office with Otto to use the phone.

"Yes," said Otto, into the phone. "Yes," he said again. "I don't know." Otto was on the phone until the end of recess.

"My mom asks a lot of questions," said Otto when he hung up at last. "I have to be home by five."

Since the day wasn't as cold as usual, Jody and Otto walked home instead of taking the bus. When they got there, Jody read his mother's note on the refrigerator, and got out the Sugar Stars cereal. He wasn't really hungry but his mother had just been grocery shopping, and when she shopped he ate all of his favorite things right away because if he waited they would be gone. Sugar Stars was Joana's favorite cereal too, and cereal boxes weren't very large.

"Gee, thanks," said Otto, when Jody offered him some. "We never have these at home because they have too many preservatives in them. My mom won't let me eat food with preservatives."

Jody was surprised. Was it possible that there were mothers worse than h:s own? Here was a mother who actually censored what her son ate. Jody poured some soda pop to go with the cereal. He was careful to eat foods with lots of protein and muscle-building vitamins, but it was different when your mother *made* you do it.

The boys finished their cereal, then went into Jody's room and closed the door. They looked at coins and Otto said he had some to trade.

After that they did pushups and lifted Jody's weights. When they sat down to rest in the living room, Otto said, "Do you know any drug addicts?"

The boys had just seen the beginning of a movie on drug abuse at school that day. In the middle of the movie the projector had broken down, and Sister Rosewitha said they would see the rest of it the next week when the machine was fixed.

"No," said Jody. "I don't know any."

"I'll bet there's a reward if you catch a real drug addict," said Otto.

Jody sat up straight at the mention of a reward. "Really? A reward?" He had seen movies with Joana about rich people who could do whatever they liked. Why, if he won the reward and became rich, he could buy his own boots and eat whatever he liked for breakfast.

"Yeah, drugs are a crime you know. If we knew of a real drug addict we could turn him in and get a reward."

"Where could we look?" said Jody.

Otto shrugged his shoulders. "I suppose they're all over," he said.

"Let's plan how we can find them," Jody said excitedly. "What do people do when they want to find someone?" he asked Otto.

The boys thought. "My mother looks in the yellow pages when she wants to find someone like a painter," Jody went on.

Otto scoffed. "Drug addicts don't advertise,

silly. They don't put ads in the paper, 'drug addicts for rent.' "

Jody frowned. This wasn't going to be easy. Drug addicts probably hid somewhere, or wore disguises.

"There are those signs on the bulletin board at the Super-Valu Market," he went on. "We could put up a notice that we're looking."

"And the guy's going to call us and turn himself in?" said Otto. "He's not going to say 'Here I am, turn me over to the police.' " Otto looked disgusted.

"No, I mean someone could call if they *knew* any drug addicts."

"If they knew, they'd turn them in themselves and get the money," said Otto. "No, we're going to have to find them ourselves. And I think the best way is to watch for them. If we see anyone that looks suspicious, like if they're carrying big bags full of pills or something, we stop them."

"When can we start?" Jody said, jumping up from his chair.

Otto looked at the clock. "I've got to go home now," he said. "But we could start tomorrow after school."

"Do we need any special equipment?" said Jody, who liked to feel professional in whatever he did.

"Naw," said Otto. "We need to keep a low image. Nothing that would attract attention. We have to look like ordinary people. Maybe just a piece of paper to write down their addresses after we follow them home so the police can arrest them."

"I've got plenty of paper," said Jody.

"OK, see you tomorrow," said Otto, as he went out the door and started home.

Just as Otto left, Jody's mother came in the back door. "Who was that leaving?" she said.

"Otto," said Jody. "He came home with me today."

"How nice," said Jody's mother. "What did you boys do?"

"Looked at coins," said Jody. "And lifted weights."

"That's nice," said his mother again.

Well, they *had* looked at coins and lifted weights. But for some reason, Jody felt guilty. He added, "We talked."

"How nice," said his mother, taking some corned beef from the freezer.

That night Jody couldn't sleep. He thought about all the money he and Otto could get by collecting drug addicts and turning them in. Why, at the post office he'd seen signs that said $5000 FOR THIS MAN. There were all kinds of pictures of men who forged checks. WANTED the signs said. Surely taking drugs was a bigger crime than forgery. The movie had made clear how serious drugs were and how illegal it was to sell them. If they could get five thousand dollars for catching a forger, surely they could get twice that much for a drug addict. "Whew!" said Jody, thinking of ten thousand dollars. He couldn't even picture that many one dollar bills. He'd never have to think about how to earn money again! One drug addict would be enough for life! And the movie had said that there were many. Even after he and Otto split the money, his share would be five thousand. He could buy some new boots (boys') and buy Joana a present and his mother new tap shoes and pounds and pounds of corned beef. He could even give a thousand dollars to St. Gertrude's and never miss it. He pictured in his mind Sister Rosewitha's face when Father Bliss announced on Sunday: "One of our own St. Gertrude's boys is a hero!" And he'd have to go up and bow, maybe even have his whole family stand up. Jody's mind wouldn't stop racing. He could see a whole new, rich, life ahead of him.

4

WHEN JODY WOKE up the next morning, his feeling of anticipation had not lessened. For the first time, he couldn't wait to go to school and get the day over with so that he and Otto could begin their work. He ran to the bus with his jacket open and his tie flying in the wind. All day he and Otto watched the clock until at last the bell rang and the boys met outside the church under the statue of St. Gertrude.

"Where should we start?" said Jody, clutching his notebook under his arm. Otto took two wheat germ cookies out of his pocket and offered them to Jody.

"I saved these from lunch," he said. "I think we should start where a lot of people go by."

Jody looked up and down the street. "No one goes by St. Gertrude's," he said.

"Naw, drug addicts wouldn't be coming to church," he said. "Maybe by the drugstore," he added. "They might get some drugs at drugstores."

That made sense to Jody.

The boys walked toward the closest shopping center. The sun was shining on their wine-colored St. Gertrude's uniforms, which were visible under their open jackets. They sat down on a wooden bench and waited.

"Here comes a lady with a shopping bag," whispered Jody.

"Let's ask her if she has drugs in her bag," said Otto. "It could be filled with drugs."

As she came closer the boys could see a head of lettuce and a carton of eggs sticking out of the top of the bag.

"She's just got groceries," said Jody.

"We don't know that," said Otto. "She

31

wouldn't put the drugs on top. They're probably in the bottom of the bag."

"But we can't ask her to dump all those things out on the sidewalk so we can see," said Jody.

While the boys talked, the lady passed by and got into her car. As she drove away, Otto said, "We need more courage than this. She probably just got away with all kinds of stuff. We let her slip through our fingers. They aren't going to come to us you know, we have to find them."

Jody was beginning to realize that apprehending drug addicts would not be easy.

"Look at that girl over there," said Otto. "She's carrying a bag."

"I think she's going to her dance lesson. She's got her shoes in that bag."

"Maybe," said Otto. "And maybe not."

Jody watched as Otto got up and walked over to the girl. He couldn't hear what they were saying, but he saw the girl swing her bag around in a circle, hitting Otto on the head. As he walked away, she called, "And I'll tell my mother and she'll go to the police and have you

locked up." Jody felt a slight shiver race down his spine. This wasn't fun anymore. It felt scary. The ten thousand dollars didn't seem as easy to get now as it did last night in bed.

Otto sat on the bench beside Jody and rubbed his head. "She had her dance shoes in that bag," he said.

Jody didn't say I told you so.

"Hey, here comes Charles Benson," said Otto.

"He's no drug addict," said Jody without enthusiasm.

"We don't know that," said Otto. "It's your turn to find out."

Jody pictured himself at home right now drawing pictures in his room. Of course, he couldn't earn ten thousand dollars drawing pictures in his room. But it was probably better than being hit over the head by Charles Benson. Reluctantly, he got up.

"Hey, Charles," he called. "What have you got in the bag?"

Charles walked up to the boys. "Jellybeans, want one?"

Jody took a black jellybean and chewed it.

"What about your pockets?" said Otto. "What do you have in your pockets?"

"None of your business," said Charles. "Why do you want to know what I have in my pockets?"

Otto poked Jody in the ribs to keep quiet. "Just wondered," he said.

Charles popped another jellybean in his mouth and walked away.

"He acted suspicious," said Otto. "Did you notice how he wouldn't tell us what he had in his pockets?"

Jody lost interest in Charles's pockets. He knew he didn't have any pills in them. "I feel hungry," he said. "Let's go over to my house and get something to eat."

"Well," said Otto, "I guess there aren't any drug addicts around here. We'll have to find a different place to look."

The boys started down the street toward Jody's house. When they got there Jody took two apples from the refrigerator and brought them to the kitchen table. They sat glumly, eating their apples and thinking.

"Hey!" said Otto, pointing. "What are those bottles on the counter?" The boys got up and went to look. Jody picked them up.

"They've got Jill's name on them," he said.

"THEY'RE PILLS!" shouted Otto.

Jody looked at the other writing on the bottles. He didn't recognize the name of the pills even with all his medical knowledge.

Otto put his hand on Jody's shoulder. In a loud whisper he said, "Your very own sister is a drug addict! We've got a drug addict in your own house! We can call the police this minute!" He walked toward the phone.

"On my own sister?" yelled Jody. "I can't call the police on my own sister. Even for ten thousand dollars!"

"It's for her own good," said Otto righteously. "We really owe it to her. Sister Rosewitha always says we are supposed to help our neighbor. We're supposed to think of others first. It wouldn't be right to let her keep doing this."

Otto threw away his apple core and picked up the bottles. He shook them. The red and green capsules bounced from side to side. He gave a long, low whistle. "These look just like the pills we saw in the movie. Those dangerous ones."

Jody had to agree they looked the same.

"Drug addicts need help. It's like they're sick," said Otto.

Jody found it hard to believe that his sister was a drug addict. Still, all the evidence was there. "Maybe we should give her another chance," he said. "I could tell my mom and she could take her somewhere for help." But when he thought about telling his mother, he changed his mind. His mother didn't like bad news. She made it very clear that the only news she ever wanted to hear was good news. He never told his mother when they had movies at school on drugs or smoking or drinking, because she called that negative reinforcement. If she found out St. Gertrude's was showing movies about negative things, she might take him out of the school and put him in another, and Jody didn't want to end up at still another school this year. At the very least she would send a note to school asking that Jody be given some artwork or history to do while the others saw the movie. He'd be the only one to be excused and probably have to go sit in the office during the movie because he couldn't stay in the classroom alone. It was against the rules. At any rate, Jody never told her. He had better talk to Jill himself.

"I think we should get rid of the pills," said Jody.

Otto was disappointed. "Here we are, handed a drug addict on a silver platter, and we let her go."

But Jody insisted, so the boys took the pills and threw them into the garbage.

"I know where there are more bottles like this," said Jody, suddenly remembering that he had seen other pills in the house. He ran into the bathroom with Otto at his heels, and opened the bathroom cabinet.

"Wow!" said Otto. "You're right, your whole family must be addicted!"

Jody remembered that sometimes his mother took a pill before she went to bed to help her sleep. Maybe it was true, maybe even his mother was an addict. The movie had said it was sometimes someone you least suspected. But his own mother? Jody knew she had strange habits, but never thought this was one of them.

Jody and Otto went through the cabinet and carried the bottles to the trash. "Gee, will they thank us for this! We're doing a good thing," said Otto.

After all the bottles had been thrown out, the boys sat down at the kitchen table and each had another apple. Jody heard Jill coming down the stairs from her room. She came into the kitchen and opened the refrigerator. She poured a glass of milk. Jody felt nervous. "Let's go to my room," he suggested to Otto, quickly getting up. Once in Jody's room, with the door shut behind them, they could hear Jill banging things around in the kitchen as if she was looking for something.

"Jody?" called Jill at last. "Have you seen the pills that were on the counter?" The boys froze.

They heard Jill come toward the bedroom. She opened the door. "OK, where are they?"

"Where are what?" said Jody in a high voice.

"My pills. They were there an hour ago, and no one else is home." Suddenly, Jill looked alarmed. "Let's see what you've got in your pockets."

Gee, thought Otto. She thinks we're drug addicts too.

"You didn't swallow them, did you?" she said.

Jody wondered how she could think he'd be that dumb when he was studying medicine.

"If you did, we'll have to have your stomachs pumped. I'll have to get both of you to the hospital." Jill was running to the phone.

"We threw them away," cried Jody in panic.

"Instead of calling the police," added Otto.

Jill turned around. "Why would you throw my pills away?" she said. "That medicine cost over ten dollars. You better find it *fast*. Do you know how mad Mom will be after what she paid for it?"

"Why would your mom buy you drugs?" said Otto. He looked alarmed.

"Because I've got a sore throat," said Jill. "And antibiotics are expensive. Where did you throw them? Go and get them this minute." Jill looked impatient.

Jody and Otto dug through the trash and found Jill's pills.

"Of all the dumb things to do," she said, getting a glass of water.

"Aren't you a drug addict?" asked Otto.

Jill choked on the water she was swallowing. "A drug addict?" she said.

Otto nodded.

"Of course not. These pills are from the doctor." When she saw Otto's red, embarrassed face, she said, "Not all pills are bad. Some pills even save lives." She patted Otto and Jody on the head and went upstairs to her room.

"I knew she wasn't a drug addict," said Jody. "Maybe it's harder to find drug addicts than we thought," he added.

Otto wasn't one to give up easily. "I think we should keep looking," he said. But the spirit was gone out of their adventure and Jody knew their big money-making plan was over. Defeated, they dug through the rest of the trash until they found the other pills and put them back in the bathroom cabinet. Then Otto said good-bye and went home.

The following week the movie projector at school was fixed, and the boys watched the rest of the film. It showed how drugs were all right if a doctor prescribed them for someone who was sick.

"They should have shown this part of the movie first," whispered Otto to Jody.

5

As soon as Jody got home from school the next day, he went to his room to change out of his uniform. Jill was there changing the sheets on his bed.

Jody knew that Jill would never tell their mother about his attempt to capture a drug addict. The children tried hard to keep news they brought home positive. If someone argued with a teacher or failed a test or fought on the playground, they were all careful to avoid mentioning it. It paid to handle problems before they got home. Drugs, of course, were high on the list of subjects that would upset their mother. And when she was upset she gave long lectures about how the world was changing and how none of these things happened when she was young. Jill found these as tiring as Jody did.

This afternoon she was unfolding a clean fresh sheet that was pink and had flowers all over it. Girls' sheets, thought Jody. His mother said flowers were not feminine and men could enjoy them as much as women, but Jody was pretty sure that men didn't have pink flowers on their sheets.

"Don't you ever touch any medicine around here again," warned Jill, tucking the sheet under the mattress.

"It was Otto's idea."

"He's a creep then," said Jill. "Well, not exactly a creep," she added, remembering Jody's shortage of friends.

As Jody was changing his uniform, a piece of paper fell out of his pocket. "We're going to be confirmed," he called to Jill, who was on her way upstairs.

She turned around and came back down. "Does Mom know?" she asked.

Jody shook his head and handed her a note.

"We have to have sponsors. The boys have to have an older brother for a sponsor."

Jill read the note from Father Bliss. "You don't have an older brother," she said.

Jody was well aware that he didn't have an older brother, or *any* brother for that matter. He didn't need reminding that he was the only man in a house with three older women.

"It says right there, we've got to have an older brother or some other male sponsor."

Jody was right, it did say that. And Father Bliss and Sister Rosewitha expected all of the children to obey the rules. Finally, he thought, his family would see how unusual they were with only one man.

"That's crazy," said Jill. "How can they be sure every boy has a brother or a father? Besides, it's sexist, the girls having women sponsors and the boys having men." Jill knew about such things.

"We have to," said Jody, as if that settled it. He was secretly glad that this flaw of his mother's had come to light. Maybe it was not too late to add another male to the family.

They heard their mother's tap shoes in the kitchen. "Mom," called Jill. "Jody's getting confirmed."

"Oh my," she said, coming into the living room. She was frowning. "I hadn't thought of that." Although Jody and his family were Catholics (they had all been baptized and received their First Communion), his mother had never made much of an issue of it and none of them had ever been confirmed.

"I need a brother," said Jody, getting out his things to draw. "By next Thursday."

Joana had come downstairs by now and was reading the piece of paper. Jody's mother was thinking hard. "We don't seem to know any Catholic boys or men," she said.

"What about Sully?" asked Jody, not really expecting a miracle. Besides, it would take years for a baby brother to grow up. He needed someone now. Sully had been very good to Jody. He had given him a Frisbee with ST. PAUL REALTY printed on it, and a big basket of fruit and nuts for the whole family when they moved into their house.

"You can't have your real estate man for a Confirmation sponsor," said Jill.

"I could be your sponsor!" said Joana suddenly. "I could dress up and look just like a boy if I tried." Joana loved to dress up. She often painted her face to look like Oscar Wilde and carried a cane, and once she dressed up like an old woman in her grandma's fur neckpiece and veiled hat, and went to the Guthrie Theater. On Halloween she dressed both herself and Jody like vaudeville actors.

Jody's mother looked interested. "Really?" she said. Joana ran up the stairs two at a time. When she came down, she had a black mustache painted on her face with a felt-tipped pen and her hair was tucked into her Greek fisherman's cap. Her necktie was fashioned from one of Jill's black knee-socks.

"Why!" said her mother. "You look exactly like a boy! Jody, look, it's the same as having a brother!"

Joana twirled her cane.

"It is NOT!" yelled Jody. "You're not coming to school like that. Mom, Joana can't be my sponsor!" He ran into his room and slammed his door.

His mother and Joana and Jill stood in a silent group outside.

"We were just kidding, Jo," called Joana.

"Yes, yes, we weren't serious," said his mother.

Jody's door opened and he came out. He looked relieved. He knew they hadn't been fooling, but he was relieved anyway when they said they were. If he wasn't careful, he knew, they'd all get carried away with the notion of dressing up and his whole family would come in costume. Anyway, he wasn't going to free his mother this easily of the responsibility of providing a real man for his Confirmation.

His mother tapped her finger against her front tooth. "We'll all have to look for a sponsor this week," she said. "Jill, you try to find one at the library. Joana, you look around school or somewhere . . . And I'll call Renee."

"I used to know a man on the school board who was Catholic," said Renee when Jody's mother called her. "Let's see, what was his name. Let me check and get back to you."

The next afternoon, Joana burst in the door after school. "I found a sponsor," she called. "My Russian teacher's brother-in-law is Catholic! She called him and he'll be glad to be a sponsor. Maybe." She added. "He only speaks Russian."

"Russians aren't usually Catholic," said her mother. "Or maybe Catholics aren't Russian. Maybe *he* isn't Russian . . . Well, I am sure he will do fine."

"I told him the day and the place," said Joana.

"Good," said her mother. "That's settled." Just then the doorbell rang.

"Mom," called Joana from the front hall. "It's another sponsor."

Her mother frowned. "Tell him to come in,"

she said. The man who came in was wearing a tweed jacket and wire-rimmed glasses. He squinted as if he read a lot in bad light.

"I am Wallace Bigelow," he said, offering his hand to Joana's mother. "I work at the reference library, and Jill said you are looking for a Catholic Confirmation sponsor."

"Dear me," said her mother, "I believe the position has been filled. Let me write your name and address down just in case we have an opening," she said, picking up a piece of paper and a pencil from the table.

"And thank you for coming!" she called after him, as he left.

"Well," said her mother, "This is more than I'd hoped for, two sponsors!"

"I think we should use my sponsor," said Joana with a bit of pout to her voice.

Her mother thought about it. "Well," she said, "we can't use both. One is really enough."

They heard Jody's school bus rumble to a stop at the end of the block. Jody got off and flew up the street and in the back door with his black tie flying. "Mom! You'll never guess what! Sister Rosewitha got me a sponsor! She said Otto's dad will be glad to be my sponsor!"

Joana clapped her hand to her forehead. "Jo, we've already got two sponsors. Otto's dad makes three."

Jody felt a quiver of excitement at this influx of males into the household. Although they were not real family, they were better than nothing. The phone rang, and their mother went to answer it. She nodded. Then she held up four fingers in the air.

"Jo, we've got *four* sponsors now."

Jody felt the way he did on his birthday when people brought him presents.

"Boy," he said. "And I was worried about not having any!"

Jody's mother hung up the phone and sat down in the green chair. She did a dance step in the air with her toe. "Renee got hold of the man on the school board. He said he would be glad to be a sponsor."

"He's not even in the running," said Joana

crossly. "I think we should take the first one that applied."

"I wish we could use them all," said Jody.

His mother seemed to agree. "I hate to turn them down," she said. "They were so good to offer."

"Well, we'll have to turn them down," said Joana.

"Unless . . ." said her mother, looking out the window. "Someone else got confirmed . . . We have three extra sponsors, and actually . . . you and Jill and I have never been confirmed . . . That's it!" Jody's mother stood up. "We will all be confirmed. That's one sponsor apiece. We won't have to turn anyone down!"

Jody was in the kitchen pouring himself a bowlful of Captain Crinch cereal. "But you need to have an older sister. Girls have to have women."

Jody's mother waved her hand in the air. "That rule doesn't apply to outsiders," she said. "Adults and public-school children are exempt." She said this with certainty and finality.

"If not, I could still wear my mustache," Joana said brightly. "We could dress like boys, since we all have men sponsors."

Jody's mother's eyebrows rose in interest.

"NO WAY," shouted Jody from the kitchen.

"We'll do it the regular way, then," she said.

And that is how Jody and his family came to be confirmed. Among the statues and Stations of the Cross, the pomp and pageantry, the bishop in his purple robe and gold miter, flanked by priests and altar boys swinging incense burners, they were all confirmed at St. Gertrude's. And Jody enjoyed every minute of not being the only boy in the family. Even for one day.

6

IN SCHOOL ONE day not long after Confirmation, Sister Rosewitha had just finished talking about honesty. The children had closed their religion books and taken out their spellers when there was a knock on the classroom door. Sister frowned, then went to speak to someone in the hall.

As soon as her back was turned, Thomas O'Toole sailed a paper airplane across the room and the rest of the class grew restless. Sister Rosewitha returned to her place in front of the desk. "I have to leave the room for a short time, and I am going to trust you to work. You are being left alone, on your honor. Remember that what you do will be between you and God. No one is to say a word to his neighbor, and no one is to leave his seat."

Sister paused and looked around the room at each child. "Do you think that I can trust you? Are you responsible enough to look after yourselves?"

There was that word *responsible* again. Jody became uneasy whenever he heard it.

"Yes, Sister," said the roomful of children, in a chorus.

"Can I leave the room knowing that everyone will be working and not disturbing his neighbor?"

"Yes, Sister," they answered in monotone.

Sister smiled. "Then let's take our spellers out and turn to page forty-eight, and I will give you your assignment to do while I'm gone."

Pages shuffled until everyone found page forty-eight.

"Write one sentence using each of the spelling words on this page. Remember your capital letters and periods. There are twenty words. That will be twenty sentences. You have plenty to do while I am gone." Smiling trustingly from child to child, Sister closed the speller and put it on her desk. Then she backed slowly out the door as if to hypnotize them into remaining in exactly the same position in which she'd left them. It reminded Jody of when Otto told his dog, Lad, to stay and then backed away slowly out of sight.

Jody looked at the first spelling word. *Equality*. Jody thought. Then he wrote, "Equality is a myth." His mother often said that. People are not equal, she said. Some are better than others. He wondered if Sister Rosewitha believed that. He didn't think so. In history class he remembered her saying, "All men are created equal." The Declaration of Independence. Jody crossed out his sentence and wrote, "The Constitution guarantees equality."

He glanced around the room. Almost everyone was writing. Brian Smith was carving his pink pet eraser industriously, but Sister hadn't said not to carve erasers. She said not to leave your seat and not to talk to your neighbor. Jody wrote another sentence. *Limited*. "The supply of corned beef was limited." He wouldn't mind some corned beef right now. He felt hungry.

Across the aisle from him, Maurice was folding a paper airplane out of a holy card. When he finished, he stood up and flew it across the room. Still, standing up wasn't leaving your seat. The airplane hit Charles Benson in the back of the neck. He stood up and said, "Who threw this?"

Someone shouted, "Maurice," and Charles walked down the aisle and pounded Maurice on the back. This was definitely leaving your seat. A scuffle ensued and Charles went back to his seat rubbing his elbow and shaking his fist. Charles told the girl across from him all the terrible things he would do to Maurice when he got him after school. This was definitely talking to your neighbor. So far Charles had left his seat and talked to his neighbor; both things he, along with the rest of the class, had told Sister he would avoid.

Jody finished the sentences on his paper. Then he closed his speller, got out a notebook and pencil, and began to draw pictures of the human body. He drew pictures of himself lifting weights, with large muscles bulging from his arm.

Before long Sister Rosewitha came back into the room. She stood in front for a moment, sliding her hands up the sleeves of her black serge habit.

"Boys and girls," she said. "May I have your attention." Everyone folded their hands on their desks at attention and looked up at Sister Rosewitha.

"Now," she said. "Did anyone leave his seat or talk to his neighbor while I was gone?"

A hush fell over the room. Not a sound could be heard except the faraway lilt of voices having music class in some distant classroom. No one raised his hand.

"Then none of you talked or left your seat?" Sister said. Jody thought about honesty and what Sister had said about telling the truth and being on your honor. She really seemed to want to know the truth. Maybe she really even *knew* the truth. Jody felt sometimes that Sister knew as much as God. Maybe she saw Charles leave his seat and talk. She didn't even need to have supernatural powers to have known that. Maybe she had never left, but had stood outside the door and watched.

Jody looked around the room. No one's hand was up.

"No one?" said Sister.

Jody impulsively raised his hand high in the air. If no one else would tell Sister that Charles talked and left his seat, he would have to. He waved his hand to attract her attention. The boys and girls all turned to look at him. Charles looked nervous. Sister seemed surprised to see Jody's waving hand. She frowned and looked a bit angry. But then her look changed and a smile came over her face. "So," she said, "Jody is the only one who is going to admit that he disobeyed. Come up here, Jody, in front of the room please."

Jody thought he'd heard wrong. *He* hadn't misbehaved. Sister was motioning him forward with her hand. She thought it was Jody who'd talked. "Come," she said. "Come up in front."

"But it wasn't *me*," mumbled Jody. "I didn't talk. It was Charles."

Sister was shaking her head from side to side and didn't appear to hear him. "It's all right," she said. "You are the only honest one in the room. Come up here now," she said sternly as Jody hesitated.

Jody walked slowly to the front of the room. Sister put her hand on his shoulder. "Boys and girls," she said. "Let this be an example to us. In the whole room, Jody was the only one who was honest about what he'd done."

Sister rummaged through her desk. "Here is a candy bar, Jody, and a blessed rosary from Lourdes."

"But I — "

Sister held up her hand, palm toward Jody, as if to hush him. "These things don't go unnoticed, boys and girls. People are rewarded for their honesty, now or in heaven. God will reward Jody, and I am sure his mother will too. Father Bliss will be very pleased when I tell him."

Jody could feel his face turning bright red. He could see Charles shaking his fist at him as he walked to his seat.

When school was over, Charles was waiting in front of the church for him. He looked angry. He also looked bigger than usual to Jody.

"You're a tattletale," he said. "A squealer." He began to pummel Jody with his fists. Jody was surprised. He saw movies on TV where people fought (just before his mother told him to change the channel) and he spent long hours in front of the mirror looking at his biceps. He lifted weights in his room to make him strong and read muscle magazines to improve his drawings of the human body. But he never ever thought that he'd have to *use* his muscles.

"Squealer," said Charles again.

Jody tried to remember how boxers stood to fight. He moved his feet around and swung his arms in the air, but he didn't feel like a fighter. And he was sure he didn't look like one. Charles mostly swung at the air too, he noticed.

Jody saw a crowd begin to gather. Suddenly

a loud, shrill voice shouted, "Hey, Charlie, you better back off before Jody uses his trapezius on you."

That was Otto's voice! Jody stopped with his arm out in midair. Charles stopped, too, at the sound of the voice, and fell forward right into Jody's outstretched arm. "OWWW," he shouted, holding his stomach.

"Hey, that was a good punch!" said Otto, coming up to Jody.

"I didn't mean to hit him," said Jody. "I hope he's not hurt."

"Hey, what did you say, Otto?" called Charles, still rubbing his stomach.

"I said you better lay off Jody. He's got a strong trapezius."

Charles's mouth fell open. He looked like he was about to say something and changed his mind.

"Yeah, well I gotta get home," he said finally, brushing himself off.

As soon as Charles was out of sight, Otto threw back his head and laughed. "He doesn't know what a trapezius is!" he said. "That scared him off."

Jody brushed off his uniform and picked up his books.

"It's good you said that right when you did," he said.

"You know something?" confided Otto. "I don't know what a trapezius is myself. I've just heard you talking about it."

"It's a muscle. Right here," said Jody, pointing to his back. "And my trapezius saved me!"

"Well, at least the name of it scared old Charlie off," said Otto.

The boys walked most of the way together, and then Jody walked on alone to his own house.

"Thanks, Otto, see you tomorrow!" he called.

Jody felt good all over. He hadn't backed down from Charles. In fact, he had stood up to him. And he did have the last punch, even if it was an accident. He ran the rest of the way home, jumping over fences and swinging from tree branches. He, Jody, who was not a fighter, had not backed down. He had not run away. He could stand up for himself. He had never known that before.

When Jody got home, he quickly ran to the bathroom and washed his face, then he combed his hair and changed his uniform. It was good that he got home before his mother did. Fighting was certainly negative. His mother must never find out about it. He would make sure of that.

By the time his mother came home, there was no evidence of a fight showing. He helped his mother carry in her books from the car.

"Maybe we should go out for supper tonight," she said. "But first you'd better wash up, Jody, you look a mess. Did you get into a fight at school?"

Jody couldn't believe his ears! She knew! How could she know?

"A little one," he said.

"I hope you didn't start it," she said, walking into her room and closing the door.

Jody sighed. There was no predicting his mother after all.

7

"WHY CAN'T I have a paper route?" cried Jody, for the fourth time in two weeks. "I want to earn money by myself. I want to work."

Jody's mother was not one to repeat herself. She had told Jody many times why he couldn't have a paper route. Now she typed it on a piece of paper and hung it on the refrigerator door. "Jody," the note said. "You may not have a paper route because it is a job that involves parents. I have to sign that I'll do the work if you don't."

"But I'll do it," Jody had said when he read that.

"Even though I know you will," she typed, as if reading his mind, "it makes me a co-worker and I don't want to be a co-worker. Love, Mom."

Jody's mother was adamant. She recognized trouble before it started. Jill advised, "Get something that's all yours, like your own business. Something you can do alone."

"I think Mom should be more supportive," said Joana when she read the note. She'd had a class in parenting in school. But she didn't talk about support when their mother was around.

Jody went outside to rake the lawn. When he had gathered a large pile of leaves and grass, he filled a plastic lawn bag. After he had filled several bags he tied them together, then sat on the steps to rest.

While he was sitting there wishing he had a job that paid money, Otto came by. He sat down on the steps beside Jody. They stared at the bags of leaves.

"I have to take these leaves to the dump," said Jody. "Want to come along?"

"How come you dump the leaves?" said Otto. "My mom runs the lawn mower over them and puts them on the garden."

"We don't have a garden," said Jody, grateful that his mother hadn't thought of that or he'd be planting and weeding and goodness knows what else in the hot sun.

"Still," said Otto, "leaves make good compost."

"Compost?" said Jody. "What's compost?"

Otto waved his hand. "It's leaves, and stuff that rots and turns into fertilizer. People buy it for their gardens."

"Buy it?" said Jody, with interest. "You mean someone would buy my leaves?"

"Well, it isn't compost yet," said Otto. "It has to be mixed with old vegetables and stuff."

"Otto," said Jody, standing up now. "Do you mean I could make compost with these leaves and sell it?"

Otto shrugged his shoulders. "I suppose," he said. "If you mixed it with a bunch of garbage and let it set around and rot for a while."

"That's it!" said Jody. "That's how I can earn money! I'll make compost and sell it! All I need is some garbage."

Jody and Otto raced back to Jody's garbage

can and opened it. They stared at the contents.

"Whew!" said Otto. "This is going to be messy. All you want is pure garbage, not cans and stuff."

The boys got the bag of leaves and shook them down. Then they bent over the garbage can and picked out old lettuce leaves and banana peels and orange rinds.

"Coffee grounds are good, too," said Otto, scooping out a handful and tossing them into the leaf bag. "And eggshells."

When they were through, they looked into the

plastic bag. "We need a lot more than this," said Otto. "Let's go over to my house and get my garbage."

The boys took an empty plastic bag and set off for Otto's house. When they got there, they began to dig through the garbage can.

"Otto?" called a voice from inside the house. "What are you doing out there?"

"We're looking for something, Mom," called Otto.

"Keep out of trouble, dear," called the voice. "And don't get your clothes dirty."

"Yes, Mom," called Otto, wiping his hand on his pants. He had encountered a particularly juicy melon rind and some orange marmalade on his third reach into the can.

"Boy, you've got lots of good stuff!" said Jody with excitement.

"But it's still not enough," said Otto, looking into the bag when they had finished. "You need enough for all the bags of leaves in your yard."

Jody looked at all the garbage cans lined up in a row down the alley. Otto saw them too. The boys went from can to can, taking only the choicest bits of tomato and the finest potato skins for their collection.

"Do you think we should ask these people if we can take their garbage?" said Jody, scraping cigarette ashes off a piece of buttered toast.

"Naw," said Otto. "Garbage is free. Anything they put out here they expect people to take."

All of a sudden Otto started to laugh. "I can just see it now," he said. "The headlines in the paper: 'Two boys arrested for theft. Reward offered for the return of ten rotten tomatoes and three pork chop bones!' " Otto was waving a limp carrot over his head and laughing.

Jody didn't laugh. Ever since the drug addict episode, he didn't see anything funny in talk about rewards. Or crime, for that matter.

By the time the boys had sifted through the contents of all the garbage cans in two blocks, they were weary. "Let's quit for today," said Jody. "This is enough garbage for the leaves I've got."

Jody said good-bye to Otto at his house, and walked on with his bulging plastic bag. When he got home, he carefully mixed equal amounts of garbage in each bag of leaves. Then he shook them. Altogether now, he had six bags of potential compost.

"And it's just a start!" said Jody to himself. "Tomorrow I'll get more."

During the next several days he and Otto collected more leaves and more garbage. Friendly neighbors whom they asked on the way said they didn't have any garbage at the moment but would bring it by Jody's house when they had some. Otto put a sign on the bulletin board at the supermarket asking for donations, and giving Jody's address.

One morning when Jody was about to leave for school, his mother began to sniff the air. "Do you smell something strange in here?"

Jody sniffed the air. "No," he said.

His mother looked into the wastebasket. Then she opened the basement door and sniffed.

"It's probably that perfume of Jill's," said Jody. "Or Joana's lip gloss that smells like bubble gum."

His mother frowned. "No, no . . . it isn't perfume or lip gloss," she said thoughtfully. Then she forgot about the smell and began to read her new library book.

At dinnertime, just as Jody and his mother and Joana sat down to eat, his mother said, "Do you smell something in here?"

"No," said Jody quickly. "I don't smell anything."

Joana sniffed the air. "Yes," said Joana. "I smell the gravy I just made. It smells good."

"No, not the gravy. I mean something else. Another smell," said their mother. "I've been noticing it all week."

"What kind of smell, Mom?" said Joana, putting some potatoes on her plate.

"Well," said their mother, "it isn't a pleasant smell."

While she was up sniffing around the cupboard, the front doorbell rang. "I'll get it, I'm up," she said.

When she came back to the kitchen, she was carrying a plastic bag. "The strangest thing just happened," she said. "A complete stranger came to the door and handed me this bag of garbage."

"That's mine, Mom," said Jody, with his mouth full of pork chop. Joana was a good cook sometimes. "It's for my compost."

"Compost?" said Jody's mother.

"Compost?" said Joana.

Jody shook his head. "I've been saving our garbage," he said. "But I needed more, for all those leaves."

Jody's mother and Joana looked out the back window. Then they went out into the yard. When they came back into the house, Jody's mother said, "As soon as dinner is over, Jody, you get rid of those bags of . . . leaves."

"Mom!" said Jody. "I can't get rid of them yet! It takes a long time to turn to compost! It has to rot some more."

Joana held her nose. "It *is* rotted," she said.

"But not enough to sell," said Jody.

"Jody, I will only say it once more. Get rid of those bags now."

Jody went to his room and threw himself on his bed. His mother was unfair. No matter what job he tried to do, she found fault with it. How could he ever earn money if his mother interfered? Jody decided it was now or never, he would simply have to stand up to his mother and demand his rights. It gave him a stomachache thinking about telling his mother that. But he had won the fight with Charles, perhaps there was a chance he could win with his mother. He felt doubtful, but he gathered his courage and walked into the living room. His mother had finished dinner and was doing her crossword puzzle.

"Mom," he said, "I think it is time I talk to you about something."

His mother looked up from the puzzle. She sighed. "What about?" she said.

"It's about my job," said Jody. "I don't think you're being fair."

Jody's mother put down the newspaper. She might be a demanding mother, but she was not an unfair person. Being called unfair bothered her.

"There isn't any job that won't involve you in some way, unless I move away from home," Jody went on.

Jody's mother looked concerned. She surely didn't want Jody to move away.

"I need a job, Mom, I need to earn money."

His mother appeared to be listening carefully, so he hurried on.

"Those bags in the yard will be gone in a few months. Can't I leave them there, please, Mom?"

Jody's mother got up out of her chair and pulled Jody down on the couch beside her. She put her arms around him and gave him a hug. "I love you lots," she said. "Do you know that?" Jody nodded. "If you want a job, we will talk about it and find something suitable. We can work out something that is agreeable to both of us, if we think about it more."

His mother did listen to him after all! "Do you mean I can keep the compost?"

His mother tapped her shoe on the coffee table. "Real compost needs more ingredients — lime, for one thing," she said. "We can think of something to do with the — er — leaves that will suit us both. Like a compromise. Let's both think."

"Do you mean where we don't keep it, but we still get money for it?"

"Exactly!" said his mother.

"The problem seems to be storing it. Our yard is too small." She wrinkled her nose. "But there's no doubt that you want to sell it, after all of your work."

Jody thought. "Maybe we need to sell it to

someone who has room to keep it and can make it into real compost." He glanced at his mother. "And doesn't mind the smell."

Jody's mother sat up. "Exactly!" she said again. "Now who could that be?"

Jody and his mother sat back on the couch and thought some more. His mother always said that being creative was being able to think. She spent lots of time thinking.

"Who could use all that compost?" she said, tapping her fingernail on her tooth.

"Someone with an awfully big garden," ventured Jody. "A real, real big one." They thought of everyone they knew with big gardens.

Suddenly Jody said, "Do you know who has he biggest garden in the whole city?"

"Who?" said his mother.

"The nursery!" said Jody. "Sullivan's Seedlings!"

"Of course!" said his mother.

"I'll call them," said Joana, who was listening in the doorway.

She ran for the phone book and looked up the

number in the yellow pages. When she came back into the living room, she announced excitedly, "Twenty cents a bag! The man will pay you twenty cents for every bag of compost you have! And he'll even come and pick them up with his truck."

"Fine!" said Jody's mother. "You see how it pays to talk about things and think them out?"

Jody had to agree that this talk with his mother was paying off in dollars and cents. But he made up his mind then and there that the next job he had would be entirely his own. It was true, his mother had helped him sell his compost quickly. But somehow, all the fun had gone out of this job. When he planned his next money-making scheme, he would not tell anyone about it, especially his mother. He would do it all on his own.

8

ONE EVENING SOON after the compost had been sold, Jody's mother wanted a Scrabble partner.

"It's your turn," Jody said to Joana. "I played Scrabble with Mom last night."

"I played last night!" said Joana. "I remember because I got *rogue* on a triple. Jill," called Joana up the stairs, "come and play Scrabble with Mom."

"Don't start arguing over who has to play with me," said Jody's mother crossly. "Why don't you all play against me, take every fourth turn."

"That's a good idea," said Joana. "I'll start."

She put down the word *vampire* using all of her letters. "Look at that! Fifty extra points!"

Their mother frowned. She used the *V* and made *vague*. "It's your turn, Jo," she said. "Put down a word."

Jody put down *biceps* and got fourteen points. Jill came down and drew seven letters.

"I think we should get a dog," said Jody's mother suddenly.

Jill looked at her. "We hate dogs," she said. "You are always telling us how they belong in the country, not the city."

"You said they smell," said Joana. "And you know who would have to take care of him."

"A dog would be good for Jody," his mother said.

"I don't like animals much," said Jody.

His mother waved her hand to discredit this. "What's there not to like? Everyone likes animals."

"I don't," said Jody.

"I'd like a cat," said Joana brightly.

"We're all allergic to cats," said her mother.

Jill put down *novel* on the Scrabble board. "Look, the *V* is double."

Her mother put down *poodle.* "If I only had an *S* I could have used almost all of my letters," she said. "What kind of a dog should we get?"

"Dogs smell," said Jill. "You run your hand over a dog's back and you smell like dog. And there would be hair all over everything. Diane had Hoover's hair on all her skirts in school last year."

"I've thought of that!" said their mother. "There are dogs that neither smell nor shed."

"And if you get one with no teeth, I'll bet he won't bite."

"Don't be sarcastic," said her mother. "We will get a dog with teeth."

"What kind doesn't smell or shed?" said Jody, putting down the word *tendon.*

"A poodle."

"Poodles are sissy dogs."

"Not standard poodles. We will get a large

dog, a standard poodle. They are as big as police dogs, and they don't shed a hair. And they don't smell."

Jody opened his mouth to remind his mother of her past attempts at raising pets, but he thought better of it. He wanted to remind her of the two ducks, Fletcher and Francis, that she brought home from a friend who lived in the country. His mother had been sure they would stay in the yard. And of the time they baby-sat Jules, Renee's St. Bernard. The trouble was, their mother lost interest in things quickly. The children had to be alert to avoid these situations.

"What is it, Jody? What were you going to say?"

Jody shook his head. "Nothing," he said. But Jody wanted to say plenty. No other mothers wanted dogs. Children wanted dogs and mothers forbade them. Jody knew he'd end up walking this dog. And feeding it after his mother tired of it.

"I won," said their mother, pushing the

Scrabble board aside. "Now let's look in the paper and see if our dog is listed."

"I heard standard poodles are rare," said Joana, looking sulky.

"So much the better!" said her mother. She liked to be different.

Jill realized they were defeated. She picked up a newspaper and paged through the want ads. She ran her finger down to PETS FOR SALE. "Lots of poodles," she said, "but they are miniature or toy."

Jody and Joana got interested. They looked through another paper.

"Here is a standard!" said Jill excitedly. She had forgotten she didn't want a dog and got swept up in the hunt. "It says, 'black standard poodle, one year old, fine self-image, telephone 738-4200.' "

Jody's mother picked up the telephone. "Do you have a black, standard poodle advertised?" she said when someone answered. Jody's mother asked a few more questions, and said yes and no a few times. "We'll be there," she said, and hung up. "We can see him tomorrow at one. He costs two hundred dollars and he's a graduate of obedience school."

"Two hundred dollars?" said Joana. "I think we should look at the pound. I'll bet we could get a dog there for ten."

"Not a standard poodle," said her mother. "Two hundred dollars seems reasonable for a standard poodle that doesn't smell or shed and has been to obedience school. I wish we could see him this minute." Their mother hated to wait for anything. Whatever she wanted, she wanted quickly.

"Tomorrow's soon enough," said Jill, thinking of how much work a dog would be. "Where is he going to sleep?" she asked her mother.

Her mother waved her hand. "There's lots of room, he can sleep anywhere."

Jill looked doubtful. "I think we should be more prepared for a dog. Get used to the idea for a while. I mean, we don't have any dog things."

"We'll play it by ear," said her mother. That's what she said often about things she wasn't ready for: We'll play it by ear.

The next afternoon while Jill and Joana were still at school, Jody and his mother drove to the address she had written on a piece of paper. "1730, 35, 1744, here it is! He said not to come early. He is scheduling appointments one-half hour apart so that Etienne doesn't get too excited."

"Etienne?" said Jody.

"It's French for Stephen."

A dog named Stephen. Jody shook his head. They sat in the car and waited until exactly one o'clock. Then they walked up the sidewalk and knocked on the door. From nowhere a large, shaggy black dog appeared, barking and growling. He slid up to the screen door, and put his head through it. His tail, with a large black puffy ball at the end of it, was wagging. Behind him, a confident gray-haired man appeared, shouting, "Heel! Etienne, heel! Sit!"

Etienne heeled. Then he sat. The man opened

the screen door, and said, "Come in, please. This is Etienne."

Etienne put his two feet on Jody's mother's shoulders and licked her face. "He gets very excited when people come," said the man. "I am Dr. Lockwood," he said, extending a hand. "He minds well, but you must be very firm. *Down, Etienne,*" said Dr. Lockwood. "Sit, Etienne."

Jody patted his head. The big dog planted his teeth over Jody's hand. "He is playful," said Dr. Lockwood. "Still somewhat of a pup. Breaks our heart to get rid of him, but we're moving to a condo, and there are no dogs allowed."

"Isn't he lovely!" said Jody's mother.

"He's active," said Jody, trying to picture him in their house. He couldn't.

"The girls will love him," said his mother. "What does he eat?"

Dr. Lockwood showed Jody's mother the organic dog food, which he purchased at a health food store, and wrote down the name of it. Then he took them out in the fenced yard and showed them how Etienne could retrieve and fetch and roll over and shake hands. "He is well trained," said Dr. Lockwood, "and he has a fine self-image. We've always allowed him to express himself." Dr. Lockwood went into the house and came back with some papers. "He's had all of his shots, and he's been neutered. These are his medical papers and his registration papers."

"We'll take him!" said Jody's mother, drawing out her checkbook and writing a check.

Dr. Lockwood and Jody loaded up Etienne's bones, balls, rings, food, bowls, automatic food dispenser, leashes, and heartworm pills. "He loves to ride in the car," said Dr. Lockwood.

The door of the car was open, and Etienne flew into the back seat like a streak. He sat tall on the seat and looked out the window, ready to go.

"Good luck!" called Dr. Lockwood as they drove away.

By the time Jill and Joana got home, Etienne had moved in. The screen on the back door was pushed out so he could see better, and every window was smudged and smeared. He ran to the window at a full gallop when he heard a voice or saw a cat or squirrel, and his toenails left large scratches on the sills.

"He's so *big*," said Joana.

Jody and his mother and Jill sat down to look at Etienne, while Joana went upstairs to change.

"He's so . . . so . . . not quiet," said Jill.

"He's just a puppy, really," said their mother. "He's barely a year old. And he's trained," she added. "Sit, Etienne!"

Etienne cocked his head to the side and put his front feet on her shoulders. "Isn't that the cutest thing!" she said. "He gave me a kiss."

"Mom, you told him to sit. I thought he was trained."

Jody's mother frowned. "When Dr. Lockwood told him to sit, he sat," she said.

"Mom," said Joana, coming down from upstairs, "he took everything out of my wastebasket, it's a mess upstairs."

"Dr. Lockwood said you must keep wastebaskets and garbage out of his reach."

"Oh fine," said Jill. "All our garbage has to be on the table, I suppose."

"Higher," said her mother. "He can reach the table. We will have to build something very high, maybe a shelf or something, for the garbage."

"I think we should train him not to get into it," said Jody.

"Too many rules could damage his self-image," said his mother.

There was a sudden knock on the door. Etienne gave a loud bark and flew to the door. He leaped into the air when Joana opened the door, and knocked Otto to the ground.

"See! See! What a watchdog!" shouted Jody's mother. "Look at that, the way he guards our house. He'll let us know when anyone comes."

Jody and Joana together held Etienne's choke chain while Otto got up. Jody went out into the back yard with Otto and shut the door.

"Mom, we can't have him knocking down everyone who comes to the door!"

"He's a fine watchdog," said her mother. "No burglars will come here."

"No friends will come either," said Jill. "And no burglars came here when we didn't have a dog."

"Preventive burglary," said her mother. "That's what a dog is for."

The next day Etienne ate a six-pack of Juicy Fruit that was on Jody's dresser. The day after that he ate the corned beef that Jody's mother had left on the counter while she answered the phone. When she drove off to the market to get more corned beef, Etienne ran to the window to watch the car drive away and tore a hole in the good lace curtains. That night, Jody's mother said, "Maybe we should let him out for a good run — without his chain on . . ."

The three looked aghast. "Mom, he'd run away!"

Jody's mother tapped her toe. She didn't say anything.

Jody rubbed Etienne's neck. "You're a good dog," he said softly.

"I think we should get rid of him," said his mother. "He's doing too much damage."

"All he needs is some discipline," said Joana, who was growing to like him a bit.

"And some manners," said Jill, "when people come to the door."

Jody's mother threw her hands up in the air. "I think he should go," she said.

"Oh, Mom, let us keep him, I'll train him," said Jody. "I'll get some books at the library."

"Good dog," said Jill, rubbing his ears.

"I don't know . . . would you promise to train him so that he doesn't eat off the counter?"

Jody nodded.

"And not tear the curtains and knock people down?"

"Yes," said Jody. Now things were as they should be. His mother was like other mothers for a minute.

"Well, he'll have a week. After that, out he goes."

Etienne walked over to their mother. He put his head in her lap.

"Oh look, Mom, he likes you."

"Well, he might be a good friend for you, Jody."

Jody hugged Etienne tightly around the neck. His mother was right. He would be a good friend. Just as soon as he trained him. He'd have a good time this summer when school was out, training him. He was a dog Jody would be proud to walk on his red leash. They could run and

play and he'd be a good friend. Dogs were man's best friend, he had heard people say.

Jody looked around at his mother and his sisters. His mother was working on her crossword puzzle. Jill was standing on her head, doing isometrics. Joana was pretending she was a dog, retrieving Etienne's blue ring on her hands and knees.

He didn't mind not having a brother. He liked his family fine. But he was glad that Etienne was a boy.